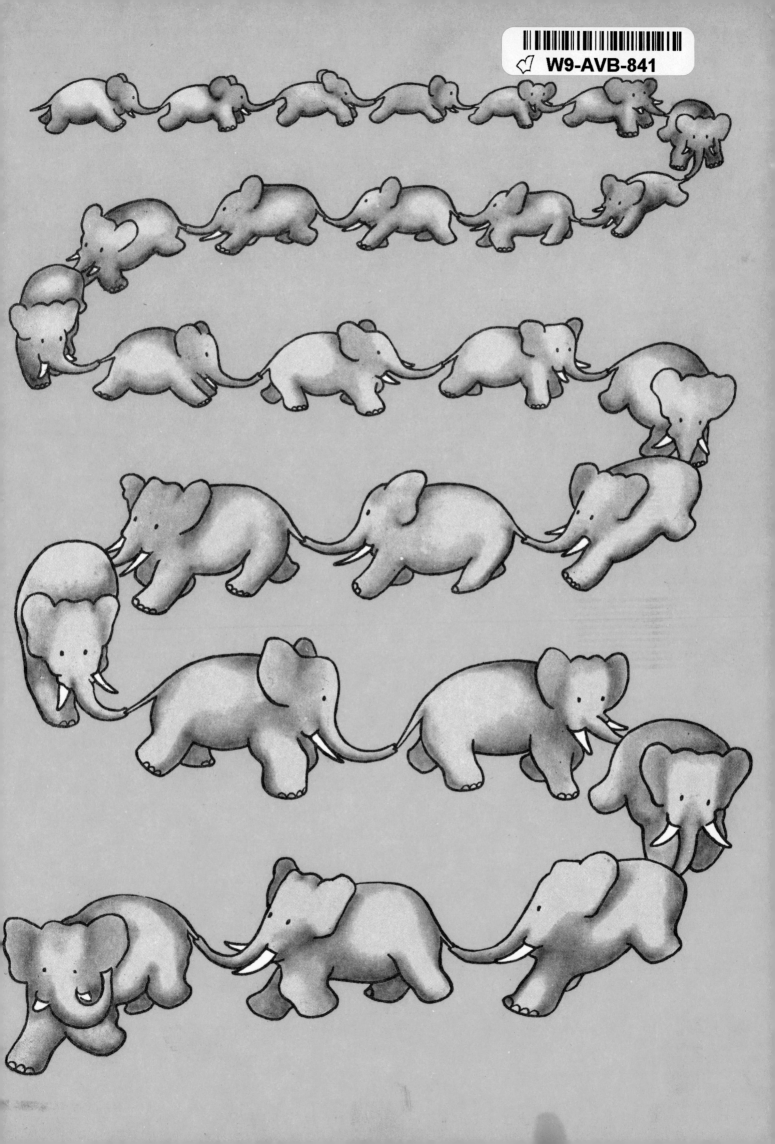

To D J
from John Glynn
Christmas 1978

BABAR AND THE WULLY-WULLY

by Laurent de Brunhoff

RANDOM HOUSE 🏠 NEW YORK

The Babar Books

The Story of Babar
The Travels of Babar
Babar the King
Babar and Zéphir
Babar and His Children
Babar and Father Christmas
Babar's Cousin: That Rascal Arthur
Babar's Picnic
Babar's Fair
Babar and the Professor
Babar's Castle
Babar's French Lessons
Babar Comes to America
Babar's Spanish Lessons
Babar Loses His Crown
Babar's Trunk
Babar's Birthday Surprise
Babar's Other Trunk
Babar Visits Another Planet
Meet Babar and His Family
Babar's Bookmobile
Babar and the Wully-Wully
Babar Saves the Day

Library of Congress Cataloging in Publication Data

Brunhoff, Laurent de, 1925- . Babar and the wully-wully. SUMMARY: Wully-Wully almost causes a war between the elephants and the rhinos, who both want the lovable creature as a pet. [1. Pets — Fiction] I. Title. PZ10.3.B7674Baaf3 [E] 75-8069 ISBN 0-394-83077-6 ISBN 0-394-93077-0 lib. bdg.

Manufactured in the United States of America   3 4 5 6 7 8 9 0

In the country of the elephants Pom, Flora and Alexander, the children of King Babar and Queen Celeste, are taking a stroll. Suddenly they find themselves face to face with a strange little animal.

"What is that?" whispers Flora.

"A Wully-Wully," answers Pom, who always knows everything.

"A what?"

"A Wully-Wully. An animal that is seldom seen."

"Let's take him home with us," says Alexander.

Flora cuddles the little animal in her arms.

"M-m-m . . ." she hums. "His fur is so soft."

In the gardens at Celesteville, the city of the elephants, Babar says, "Yes, this is certainly a Wully-Wully. He is very gentle-looking and quite lovable."

The Old Lady, a close friend of the Babar family, smiles fondly

at the small creature, but Zephir the monkey acts reserved. Babar's young cousin Arthur quickly takes some photos.

"My goodness!" exclaims old General Cornelius, "What an event! I haven't seen a Wully-Wully in almost ten years."

The Wully-Wully has
a very good time
in Babar's house.
The toys of Pom, Flora
and Alexander fascinate
him, especially
the electric train. He
watches it go around
him hour after hour.

Wully-Wully also likes to play hide-and-seek.
He steals off quietly and hides in all sorts of places—
in a drawer . . . behind the drapes. . . . He is difficult
to find because he makes no more noise than a feather.

The Wully-Wully eats with the rest of the family, but instead of sitting down with them he prefers to hang upside-down by his tail. He also sleeps in that position—like a bat.

Wully-Wully is really very happy in Celesteville. Every day he discovers astonishing new things. Arthur teaches him to blow into a saxophone. Wully-Wully makes some loud squawks and everybody bursts out laughing.

But Wully-Wully likes
the country even better,
so the children take him
on a picnic. While they
are unpacking the food,
Rataxes the rhinoceros
is spying on them.

"A Wully-Wully!" he says.
"If I can snatch him away,
he'll be mine!"

The little pet suspects
nothing, and neither do the
children.

Suddenly Rataxes jumps out from behind the bush, shoves
the little elephants out of the way, and seizes the Wully-Wully,
who lets out a piercing cry. But what can he do against a huge
rhinoceros?

Rataxes jumps into his car with the Wully-Wully and drives off, laughing loudly. Arthur and the others try to chase after him, but the thief gets away. They are all in despair. They think they have lost their little Wully-Wully forever.

They rush back to the garden to find Zephir.
"You must help us," says Pom.

After he has heard the whole story, the little monkey says, "Arthur, let's go on a search."

The two scouts creep up to the city of the rhinos. Zephir looks through his binoculars.

He can see the little Wully-Wully tied by a leash. Rataxes doesn't let him loose for an instant.

To get closer to the city without being seen, Arthur puts on one of his disguises.

Dressed like a camel, he walks behind the bushes. Zephir looks like someone out for a ride.

They see that Wully-Wully looks very unhappy. "How can we save him?" Arthur asks.

"Just you wait, Rataxes," threatens Zephir. "I am going to think up a trick to get into your city."

Later that day a strange hat merchant arrives in the city of the rhinos. Everybody rushes to the city square for the rhinos all adore hats.

Suddenly Rataxes cries: "Arthur, you rascal! *I* recognize you! A hat merchant indeed! You want to take back the Wully-Wully, don't you? But you can't fool me. It's off to prison for *you!*"

In the garden at Celesteville Pom, Flora and Alexander are waiting. Zephir promised to be back with the Wully-Wully in two hours.

Alexander climbs to the top of a tree to watch for their arrival, but no one comes. The road is empty.

The hours pass.
Flora begins to cry.
Pom comforts her.
"Come," he says,
"let's find Papa."

That evening everybody is very worried. Cornelius plays cards, but he cannot hide his concern. "You never know what that Rataxes will do," he says. The Old Lady agrees.

Babar tries to reassure them. "You just wait," he says. "Arthur and Zephir will be successful. Don't worry."

The children go to bed. But Flora cannot sleep. She is too sad.

All this time Arthur has been shut up in a tiny, dark cell. Fortunately Rataxes did not catch Zephir. The clever monkey managed to get away and is hiding near by. As soon as darkness falls, he runs up to the prison and shouts:

"Arthur! I am going to save you! Have courage!"
The guards, outraged by this impudence, chase after him.

It's easy for Zephir to lead the clumsy rhinos away from the prison. They puff along behind him, shouting: "Beware, you monkey! We'll fix you!"

Suddenly, without knowing how it happened, the guards lose all trace of Zephir.
Where has he gone?
They can't believe it!

After leading the guards astray Zephir quickly goes back to the prison. He gets the door open.

Arthur is free!

While Arthur hides in the woods, Zephir runs to the palace. "I am going to set the Wully-Wully free," he says, "before someone gives the alarm."

Quietly as a cat Zephir creeps inside Rataxes' palace. Arthur watches him vanish right under the noses of the sleeping guards.

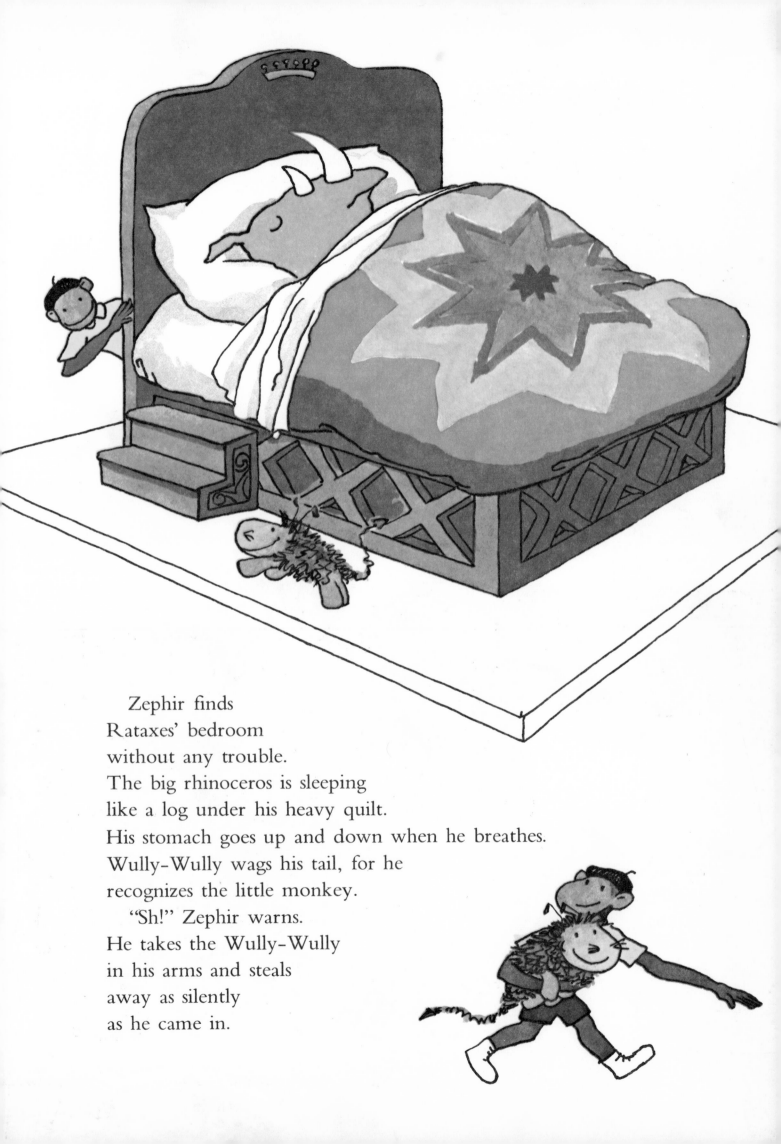

Zephir finds
Rataxes' bedroom
without any trouble.
The big rhinoceros is sleeping
like a log under his heavy quilt.
His stomach goes up and down when he breathes.
Wully-Wully wags his tail, for he
recognizes the little monkey.
   "Sh!" Zephir warns.
He takes the Wully-Wully
in his arms and steals
away as silently
as he came in.

Zephir and the Wully-Wully
find Arthur and, without
losing a second, all three
of them leave the city.
Soon they are far away,
and Zephir begins to chuckle.
"Rataxes is going to make
a funny face when he wakes up!"

Very early in the morning Babar and Celeste hear shouts under
their windows. Everybody rushes out to greet the returning heroes,
who are very proud of their escapade.

"Good gracious!" exclaims The Old Lady. "What a relief! I didn't
sleep all night." And Flora hugs her Wully-Wully.

The news spreads very fast through Celesteville. The elephants gather to congratulate Arthur and Zephir. They carry them in triumph through the streets.

"Bravo, Arthur! Bravo, Zephir!" they shout. "You have outwitted Rataxes! Bravo! Long live the Wully-Wully."

Pom, Flora and Alexander go off by themselves, taking the Wully-Wully with them.

"Tell us all about it, Wully," says Flora while scratching her pet's back. Wully-Wully twitches his whiskers and smiles.

But suddenly— they hear a frightful rumbling like an earthquake!

It is Rataxes and his rhinos, sweeping through Celesteville like
a hurricane. The elephants are so stunned by this terrible charge

that they cannot even resist. The rhinos disappear in a cloud of dust, carrying Wully-Wully away with them.

Babar immediately calls all the elephants together. Cornelius and his soldiers stand beside him. The elephants are furious. They shout: "Down with Rataxes! Let's go after the thieves! We want to fight!"

Babar does not want to go to war, but what can he do?

Little Flora is worried.
She starts thinking:
    "If there is a war
with the rhinos, what
will happen to Wully?
He could be killed.
And if he dies,
there will be no more
Wully-Wully."

Flora decides that she will go to find Rataxes. "I will explain all this to him," she thinks.

Without saying anything to anyone, she leaves Celesteville. As fast as she can go, she runs straight to the city of the rhinos.

When the guards bring the spunky little elephant to Rataxes the fierce old rhinoceros scowls and says:

"What have you come here for? Aren't you afraid?"

"Why should I be?" asks Flora.

"Well, you know that Arthur and Zephir played a trick on me!" says Rataxes.

Flora does not answer. Instead she asks:

"Why do you keep poor Wully-Wully in a cage? And why did you steal him? He is not yours."

"He is not yours either!" grumbles Rataxes.

"You are right. He isn't really mine. But I am the one who found him and I never tied him up. I didn't put him in a cage either, yet he stayed with me."

Perplexed, Rataxes scratches his ear. "If I let him out of the cage he will run away."

"Perhaps," says Flora, "but he will come back when he wants to."

Still troubled, Rataxes opens the cage.

"Little girl," he says, "I think you are trying to twist me around your little trunk."

Now the Wully-Wully can go where he wishes. Each day he usually stops to see Flora and the elephants, but he also visits in the city of the rhinos. When Wully-Wully is at Celesteville, Rataxes is likely to be there too, helping Flora make a rope swing for the little pet.

Babar watches them and thinks, "It's really amazing. Our little Flora has completely tamed the great, rough Rataxes!"

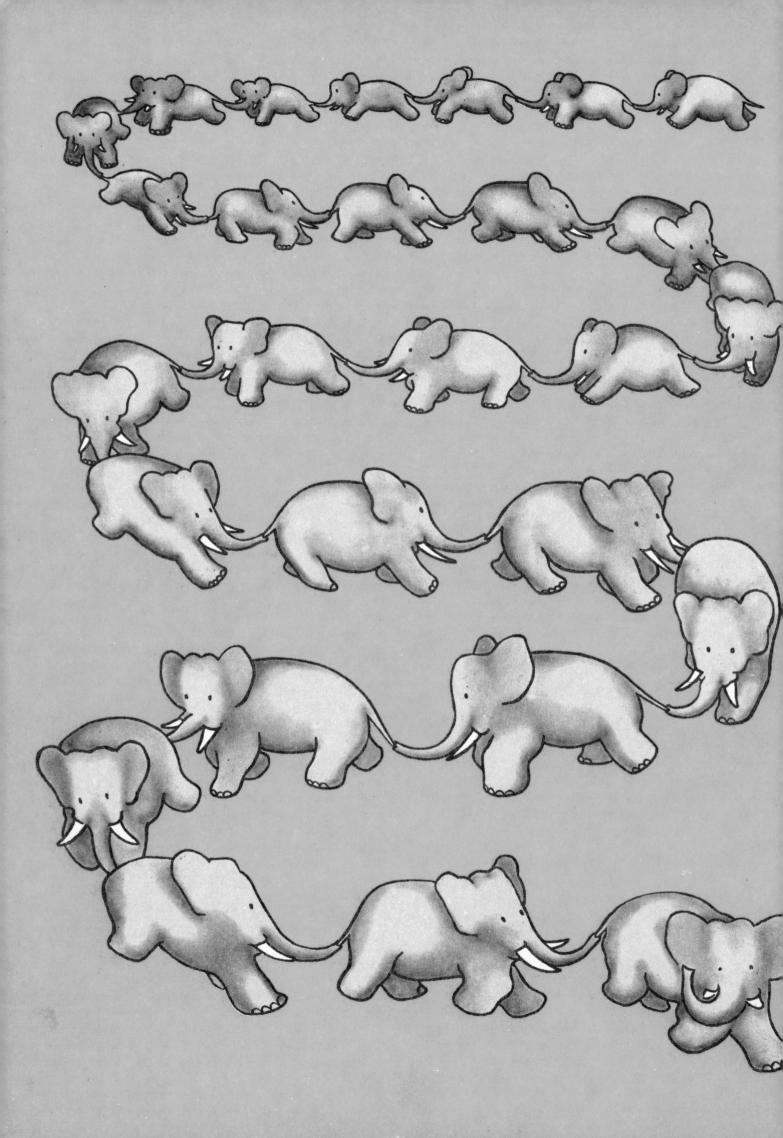